Good Morning, Chick

adapted from a story by Korney Chukovsky

by Mirra Ginsburg
pictures by Byron Barton

GREENWILLOW BOOKS, New York

TO ALIK OSIK

Text copyright © 1980 by Mirra Ginsburg. Illustrations copyright © 1980 by Byron Barton. Text adapted from the Russian *Tsyplenok* by Korney Chukovsky.
All rights reserved. No part of this book may be reproduced without permission from Greenwillow Books, 1350 Avenue of the Americas, New York, NY 10019.
Printed in U.S.A.   12 11 10 9 8 7
Library of Congress Cataloging in Publication Data   Ginsburg, Mirra. Good Morning, Chick.   1. Chickens—Fiction I. Barton, Byron.
II. Chukovskii, Kornei Ivanovich, 1882-1969. III. Title PZ7.G43896Go   [E] 80-11352   ISBN 0-688-80284-2 (trade). ISBN 0-688-84284-4 (lib. bdg.)

There was a little house
White and smooth

One morning, tap-tap and crack!
The house split open

And a chick came out.
He was small and yellow and fluffy

With a yellow beak
And yellow feet

His mother's name was Speckled Hen.
She looked

like this

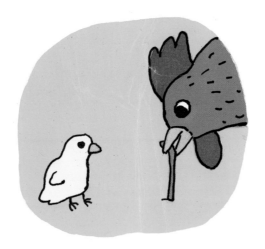

She loved the chick
And taught him to eat worms
And seeds and crumbs,
Peck-peck, peck-peck, peck-peck

like this

A big black cat jumped out
Of the house and hissed
At the chick

like this

The Speckled Hen spread out her wings
And covered the chick like this.
"Cluck-cluck-cluck!" she scolded,
And the cat backed away

like this

Then a rooster flew up on the fence,
Stretched his neck, and sang,
"Cock-a-doodle-do!"

like this

"That's easy," said the chick.
"I can do it too."
He flapped his wings
And ran.
He stretched his neck
And opened his beak

like this

peep
peep

But all that came out
Of his beak was a tiny little
"Peep! Peep!"
He didn't look where he was going
And he fell into a puddle,
Plop!

like this

A frog sat in the puddle and laughed,
"Qua-ha! Wait till you grow
Before you can crow!"
The frog looked

And the wet chick looked

like this

Now Speckled Hen ran to her chick.
She warmed and coddled him

like this

The chick dried out
And was round and golden and fluffy again.
And off they went together
To look for worms and crumbs and seeds.
Peck-peck, peck-peck, peck-peck

like this

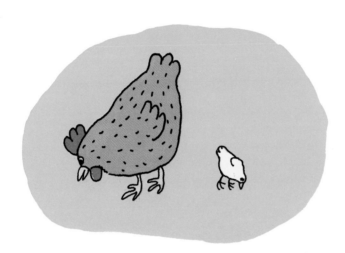